D1577356

Contents

Acknowledgment: Endpaper illustration by James Hodgson.

The Yellow Book of bedtime stories

Ladybird Books
Loughborough

The moth and the mirror

by Charlie Chester
illustrated by James Hodgson

All the insects in the forest have a king to rule over them, to see that they behave nicely and do their work properly. (All except the butterflies – they have a queen instead.)

Now the king of the moths was a beautiful specimen. He had enormous wings, and was the biggest moth that anyone ever saw.

He flew in and out of the forest to make sure that all the other moths were being looked after all right; in fact, he was busy from early morning until very late at night.

One day King Moth flew out of the forest and went in search of some houses, where he hoped to find some work for some of the other little moths. As he fluttered around in the dusk, it started to rain. Naturally he didn't want to get his wings all wet, and as it began to thunder, he made his way to a big mansion.

He fluttered outside the window for a moment, then, just before someone closed the window, he popped inside and settled for a while on the ceiling.

He admired the furniture and the carpets and all the lovely things inside the mansion. Then, as he sat there, it slowly got darker until it was quite dusk. Now there were shadows everywhere and it was time to search the mansion. King Moth left the ceiling and flew through the great hall into a large bedroom.

What a sight greeted his eyes . . . an enormous bed with a rich canopy over it. Velvety curtains and thick carpeting . . . then, a strange thing happened . . . suddenly, in the shadows, King Moth saw something . . . he couldn't believe his eyes . . . it was another moth . . . a beautiful moth . . . the most beautiful creature he had ever seen . . . and he fell in love with it right away. Every time he fluttered a little nearer, she seemed to do the same . . . oh, she was so lovely! King Moth thought to himself, this is the moth that must be my Queen. What poor King Moth didn't know was that he was seeing his own reflection in the large mirror. Being a moth he wasn't to know that . . . and he was so happy to have found someone so beautiful to be his Queen.

Suddenly the storm grew worse, and lightning struck the mirror . . . it cracked and fell to pieces. As the mirror

fell to the floor, the reflection of King Moth disappeared too . . . oh dear, he was heartbroken! To think that he had found the perfect moth to be his partner and then to have her disappear like that!

Wherever did she go? he thought. She was there a moment ago, she couldn't just disappear into thin air . . . she must be here somewhere . . . and he flew all over the mansion in search of her . . . but however hard he looked he could not find her. At last, in despair, he went back to the forest and called a special meeting of all the other moths.

He told them what had happened . . . how he had seen the most beautiful moth in the world . . . and how he had fallen in love . . . and that he wanted to marry the beautiful creature he had seen.

Then he told them all how she had disappeared . . . he explained that one moment she was there . . . and the next moment, with a flash of light, she had disappeared. He distinctly remembered the flash of light . . . it was very bright. He felt sure that the light must have had something to do with it.

All the other moths listened intently to their King Moth. They were very sad that he should be so unhappy . . . and besides, they were anxious too that they should have a lovely Queen.

They decided that the special beautiful moth must be found . . . and they flew everywhere in search of her . . . but none could find her. Then they decided that the light must be important, and the King decreed that every moth should search not only the darkness but especially the light to find her.

They are still searching to this day to find the moth that disappeared in a flash of light. That is why you will always see a moth flying around the light, or even a candle flame . . . they even get burned in their efforts to find the Queen Moth that never was . . . for she was only a reflection of King Moth in the mirror.

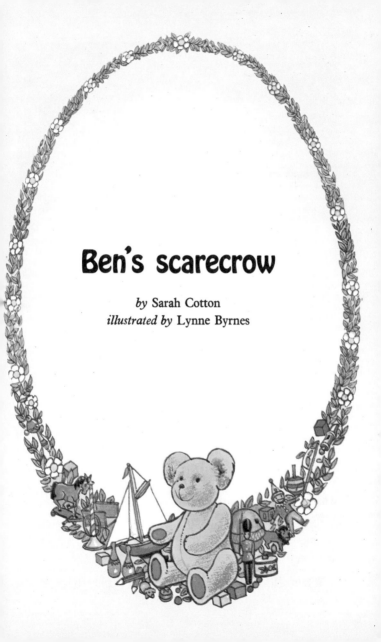

Ben's scarecrow

by Sarah Cotton
illustrated by Lynne Byrnes

One morning when Ben went out to look at his garden, to see whether the beans were growing taller or the peas fatter, he heard a cluck clucking noise. In fact, quite a lot of cluck clucking noises.

Then he saw what it was. The naughty hens, led by Horatio the cockerel, had jumped over the fence. They were having a second breakfast on Ben's peas and beans and his wriggly worms that were so good for the earth. He was very cross.

"Shoo, shoo, you naughty hens, get out of my garden at once!" he called, running towards them and waving his arms in the air to frighten them away.

When Horatio and his hens were safely back in the

orchard, Ben realised he had a problem. How was he to stop Horatio and his hens from eating all the vegetables?

There was already a fence round the garden, so there didn't seem much point in having another one, and he certainly couldn't stand around all day making sure they behaved themselves.

Then he had an idea. *He* couldn't stand around all day, but someone else could! That was the answer. He would make a scarecrow and stand it in the middle of the garden.

He hurried indoors and went up to his bedroom. He looked at his dungarees, the ones that his mother had patched and were really far too small and decided to ask whether they could be used for his scarecrow. Then he would need a shirt, jacket or cardigan and a hat. After all, if you are going to be a scarecrow standing all alone day after day, night after night, you have to be warmly dressed!

Downstairs he found his mother. "I'm going to make a scarecrow to keep the hens away from my garden. May I use these old dungarees?" he asked. "They are getting very small."

"Of course you can," said his mother. She thought for a moment, then said, "If you go to the cupboard under the stairs you will find my rag-bag. Bring it here and we'll see if there's anything suitable in it."

Ben found the bag and together they turned everything out. "There's Daddy's old cardigan and my striped pyjama jacket. That would do for a shirt. May I have them both, please?"

"Yes, take them, and what about this scarf? Is that any good to you?" asked his mother, handing it to him. Ben was delighted. Now he had everything, except for a hat.

His father came in and asked what all the clothes were for. Ben explained.

His father thought it was a very good idea, and asked him, "Do you need anything else ?"

"Only a hat," replied Ben.

"Would a cap be any good ?" asked his father.

"Oh yes !" replied Ben.

"There's my old check one. I think it's hanging in the cupboard under the stairs on one of the pegs. Have a look, anyway."

"Take the rag-bag and put it away at the same time," Ben's mother reminded him.

Ben found the cap. It would be perfect. Now he had everything he needed.

13

He took the clothes and hat out into the garden. Leaving them in a pile in the garage, he went in search of one more thing. He needed two long sticks. He found them easily, as his father had told him he could use the bean poles that he kept behind the garden shed when they were not being used for the bean plants to climb up. He chose two that were almost the same size, and took them to the garage. Laying them down in the shape of a cross, he carefully hammered a nail through them to join them together.

Now to dress his scarecrow! First of all, he put the upright pole through one leg of his old dungarees, and tied the waist on tightly half-way up the pole. Then he put the pyjama jacket on so that the pole across went through the sleeves, and stuffed them full of old straw he had brought from the shed by the orchard. Next, he stuffed the trouser legs the same way. He had to use a lot of straw to fill the second trouser leg, to make it look like a proper leg, but when he had finished he was very pleased. Then he carefully fitted his father's cardigan over the pyjama jacket shirt and tied the woolly scarf round the scarecrow's neck. Last of all, he stuck his father's old check cap on top of the pole.

He stood back to look at his handiwork. It wasn't quite as he had expected it to look. In fact, something was wrong. For a moment Ben was puzzled, then he had an idea. He went into the orchard, and climbed over the fence into the field. Soon he was running across the field to Mr Evans the farmer, who was busy milking the cows in the milking parlour.

"Be with you in a minute, young man," he shouted as he caught sight of Ben. "Stay where you are."

Ben stayed where he was.

When Mr Evans had finished milking one of his cows he came over to Ben, who quickly explained about the chickens in his garden and how he was making a scarecrow. Mr Evans smiled when he heard Ben's problem.

"Come with me, Ben," he said, leading the way to a barn. It was quite dark inside. But once Ben got used to the dim light he could make out a big pile of swedes in the corner.

"Would this one be about right ?" Mr Evans asked Ben.

"I should think your father's cap would fit nicely on this one."

"Oh yes, thank you very much indeed," said Ben happily. "You will come and see my scarecrow when I've finished it, won't you?"

"I'll be up later," promised Mr Evans. "Right now though I must get back to my cows."

Ben went home across the field, climbed over the fence into the orchard and went back to his scarecrow. He tried first to put the swede on top of the pole, but it was much too hard, so he went to get a knife. His mother suggested he use the potato peeler.

"You'll be able to make a big hole with that," she said.

Ben cut out a big hole, big enough to fit on top of the stick. He put the swede head in place, then put the check cap on it. Only one more problem – how to get the scarecrow from the garage into the garden.

His father came into the garage at that moment, for he knew Ben would need some help. Carefully they carried the scarecrow into the vegetable garden and stood him in the middle of Ben's patch. He looked rather splendid. He had a striped pyjama shirt, patched blue dungarees, a red cardigan, a spotted scarf and a check cap on top of his swede head.

Ben was very proud of him. "I do hope he does the trick and keeps Horatio and the hens out," he said to his father.

"Well, we can only wait and see," replied his father.

Ben *did* wait and see. Next morning he was very pleased as naughty Horatio and his hens took one look at the well-dressed scarecrow, and never again dared to go into Ben's garden to eat wriggly worms or to steal his peas and beans!

Hopper

by Hazel Wood
illustrated by Brian Price Thomas

Hopper was the most beautiful grasshopper in his garden. He had his own corner of the garden to live in, with plenty of friends and neighbours all within two or three hops, so he was never lonely. He was liked by nearly all the other grasshoppers in the garden, although one or two of the older ones did not have much time for him because Hopper was always daydreaming. He would sit quietly in the warm sunshine, dreaming that he was travelling all over the world, doing good wherever he went. Or he would dream that he was fighting enemy grasshoppers who were

trying to kill his friends. And of course he always won his fights, no matter how strong his enemies were! Sometimes his dreams seemed so real to Hopper that he believed they had actually happened, and he just couldn't wait to tell his friends and neighbours of his latest 'adventure'. Then they all smiled, because they knew he'd been dreaming again. Everyone around knew Hopper had the best hopping legs in the garden, so he was often asked to help the older grasshoppers when they needed something done in a hurry.

Hopper was sitting in his corner of the garden one warm afternoon, resting after his dinner, when the quiet was disturbed by loud crunching noises. Hopper became uneasy and turned to see what was making the noise. What a shock! Humans were coming. Hopper thought he had better warn his friends to stay hidden in case they got hurt or even squashed! He went jumping all over the garden shouting as loudly as he could, "Stay inside, humans are coming. People about – stay inside." Soon word spread and the only grasshopper to be seen was Hopper. There were humans everywhere: big ones, even bigger ones, small ones and even one tiny one. Now Hopper had a problem: he had to get home himself.

He jumped and jumped, trying to make each hop bigger so that he would be home and safe as quickly as possible. Not far to go now. Hopper was almost home when all of a sudden, something happened. The light had gone, the grass had gone, and he couldn't hear anything. He knew he was moving, although his legs were still. Now Hopper was really frightened. He shouted as loudly as he could for help, though he knew that none of his friends could help, for what could *they* do against humans?

The movement stopped for a moment, then all at once, without warning, Hopper was dropped into a funny glass jar. There was grass covering the bottom, and through the sides he could see out to his garden. He could even see his home, but although he jumped and hopped as hard as he could, something stopped him from getting back. At the top there were tiny holes in the ceiling. They let air in, but they were not big enough to crawl through. Then the glass jar moved again as all the humans started walking away from the garden. Hopper was bumped up and down for ages and ages. He tried his hardest to hang onto the glass walls, but soon had to give up. He was very lonely and very upset. His adventure had tired him out completely. He tried to keep awake but it was just too much for him. Soon he was sleeping deeply on the soft grass.

When Hopper awoke his glass jar was quite still. He felt hot and rather hungry, and didn't realise where he was until a human face came right up to the glass. It looked enormous, and Hopper was terrified. Then he felt he was moving again, being lifted high somewhere. When he looked through the glass, he was inside a great big room, with small humans everywhere! There was one big human, and she was holding up Hopper's glass jar for the little humans to look at. For several minutes Hopper was held high while the big human was talking, then she put the glass jar down on the table. Hopper felt much safer when the jar was still.

Then the worst part of this whole terrible adventure started. To Hopper it seemed to go on for hours, but it was probably only about half an hour. Four faces at a time peered in at him. He hopped round and round to find somewhere safe where there wouldn't be a human face staring at him, but there was nowhere to hide. And every time he hopped, the small humans laughed or screamed.

Hopper by now had had enough adventure to last him his lifetime! The only thing he wanted was to get out of this glass jar. Even if he couldn't find his way home to his corner of the garden, at least he would be free.

The small humans were putting their coats on, and Hopper could see some big humans outside, looking into the building. "Well, *they* are lucky enough to be free – I wish I was," he said to himself unhappily. "I bet *they* wouldn't like being kept in here." Then once more he was lifted high and pushed down into something dark. Hopper did not know quite what was happening, but he did know he was moving again, for he was shaken and jolted about even more than before.

He was in the dark for what seemed like ages, his tummy still hungry and his mouth still thirsty. Then all at once he could see again, as his glass jar was put down outside. Hopper looked through the glass and saw his garden, "My shed, my garden," he thought happily, then realised he wouldn't be able to hop about with his friends. As he looked out sadly, Hopper suddenly felt the grass sliding up the wall of the glass jar. He was carefully tipped out, grass and all, onto the garden path. Like lightning Hopper was off.

His friends had been watching the humans and were amazed to see them bring Hopper back. Grasshoppers appeared from everywhere wanting to know what had happened, but all Hopper wanted was his nice quiet corner of the garden and something to eat. Hopper had had enough of adventures, and who would believe him if he told them anyway?

The Nativity play

by Bette L. Vickers
illustrated by Jonathan Langley

One mild winter a few years ago, when all it seemed to do was rain, Deirdre the donkey was staying with the Jenkins family.

It was quite a large family. There were Mr and Mrs Jenkins, there were Lucy, Polly and Mary, the three girls, and two boys: Paul and David.

They all lived in a large stone cottage in a big village called Haltham. Mr Jenkins worked on a farming estate and looked after the cows. This meant he had to get up very early for milking time, and he also had to work nearly every weekend.

Sometimes, when he had a week-end off, Mr Jenkins would take all the family out for a day to the seaside or the zoo, or on a picnic.

Deirdre had gone to stay with the family for the winter months, for there was plenty of room for her in the stables and fields. At night when the weather turned colder, or if it rained during the day, she was put in a lovely dry stable which was filled with soft straw. Everyone looked after her, and the children enjoyed having her.

Every year the young people of Haltham and their parents all worked hard to raise money for a Christmas Party for the old people who lived in the village. Coffee mornings, bazaars and jumble sales were all organised to raise money for food, decorations and presents. And, of course, a large Christmas Tree!

The Jenkins boys and girls had always been too young to help, and sometimes they felt a little left out of things when everyone else was working so hard.

One night as the girls lay in bed, Polly said, "I do wish we could do something for the Christmas Party – it would be nice to feel we were helping for a change."

"Yes, it would," answered Lucy, "but what can *we* do?"

"The trouble is, Mummy is always so busy at this time that we only get in the way," Mary sighed. They all three went deep in thought before, at last, they fell asleep.

Next day on the way to school, the girls told Paul and David how much they would like to be part of the Christmas celebrations.

"Well, it *would* be nice, but I can't think what we could do," said David.

"No, I can't either," said Paul, who was the eldest. "We shall just have to wait until we are older."

Polly was not going to be put off, however. During the next few days she gave the matter a great deal of thought, but no matter how she tried, she just couldn't think of a single idea that would work.

Every day on their way home from school, the children stopped to chat to Deirdre for a while. She loved to see them and would come to the gate to have her nose rubbed.

On this particular day, they climbed the gate and sat on it swinging their legs.

And that's when Polly had her brilliant idea!

"I know what we can do!" she said, scrambling down from the gate.

"Do for what?" said Paul, puzzled.

"Why – the Christmas Party, of course," she replied.

"Oh – *that*," said Mary. "I'll bet they won't let us do whatever you've thought of."

"Yes, they will – if we can do it properly, that is."

"Well, what *is* this great idea?" Paul asked.

"A Christmas play," answered Polly. "You know, like the Nativity play we do at school, all about when Jesus was born."

"Don't be silly," said David. "There aren't enough of us, and we don't have any costumes to do it with anyway."

"We can always ask some of our friends to join in – like Robert Sharpe and Jane Strong for instance," ventured Lucy.

"You see!" said Polly. "We *can* do it if we try."

The boys and Mary began to get interested and when they asked Jane and Robert to join in everyone was delighted when they said yes.

Then at last they told Mummy of their wonderful idea, but she didn't think it was a very good one. The children were so disappointed that at last she said, "Oh, all right then. Let's see what you can do."

So the children asked for old clothes to make costumes. They collected dresses, sheets and blankets and used them for shepherds, angels and all the costumes they needed.

They talked it over and decided that Paul would play Joseph and Polly would play Mary.

The children became more and more excited as the great day drew near. One morning, at breakfast, they were chattering so much about their rehearsals that Daddy said, "Do calm down now – you'll be giving old Deirdre a part next!"

"Oooooooooooooooooh!" cried Polly. "What a *super* idea! She can be *the* donkey and carry Mary to Bethlehem."

Daddy laughed. "I was only joking," he said, "but why not have a try and see what happens?"

And they did!

They took Deirdre to the big barn and Polly climbed onto her back. Then they led her to the stage they had

made and showed her what to do. After a few rehearsals Deirdre became so good that everyone started clapping.

Deirdre did not realise what was happening of course, but she knew it was something special, and she was on her best behaviour.

And at long last, the great day arrived. It was a wonderful party, and the old people enjoyed every moment.

As soon as they had all had tea, the vicar announced, "Now we have a special treat for you. It is a Nativity play, given by a group of children who have written and produced it all by themselves."

They were on!

The play was going very well indeed. Deirdre waited behind the door of the barn with Polly and Paul, until it was time to walk down to the stage, where straw had been placed for the stable of the inn.

As the little procession moved, Deirdre walked very slowly and regally with Polly, dressed all in blue, on her back.

The audience gasped when they saw a real live donkey, and were amazed at how good it was being.

When the procession reached the stage, Paul helped Polly down from Deirdre's back. Then he spoke to the inn-keeper who showed them to the stable on stage.

Mary and Joseph sat down on the straw with the donkey standing behind them. The little group made a lovely picture and made the story come to life for the people watching.

But what do you think happened then? The warmth of the straw, the lights and the heated barn all became too much for Deirdre. She lay down and fell asleep! Right there on the stage!

The children carried on as if nothing had happened. After all, perhaps the donkey *did* fall asleep on the night that Jesus was born. When the play was finished the people clapped and clapped, and even cheered.

The noise woke Deirdre and she stumbled to her feet. She looked a little puzzled and worried – she knew she shouldn't have fallen asleep, but the children soon showed her that it didn't matter.

"Oh Deirdre, you were so good!" said Polly.

"Yes, and it was so funny when you fell asleep," said Paul.

They hugged her and led her to the Christmas tree where the presents were being given out. There was a large bunch of carrots for Deirdre, tied up with a shiny red ribbon.

There was a card too, with a picture of a donkey on the front who looked very like Deirdre herself.

The card said, "To Deirdre, the best donkey in the world. May you have a Happy Christmas."

And she did.

The very clean pig

by Moira Smith
illustrated by Martin Aitchison

Percival Pig was a very clean pig indeed. He was the cleanest pig you could ever meet. When he was born, with his six brothers and sisters, he was the pinkest pig his mother had ever set eyes on. Then as he got older, Percy's mother noticed that he was not behaving at all like a pig. "He seems different from his brothers and sisters," she thought. "He's becoming too stuck-up for his own good. I can't think where he gets his ideas from!"

Percy's brothers and sisters all had names like 'Porkie' and 'Pinkie', but Percy made his family and friends call him 'Percival'. "Strangers may call me 'Percival Pig Esq'," he said. He wasn't sure what 'Esq' meant, but he thought it sounded very good.

Each morning, when the other pigs snorted and rushed to roll in the mud, Percy slowly washed himself in the trough instead. He even washed behind his ears. Of course he always had his morning drink of water first.

When the pigs grew older, Percy said one day, "I'm sorry, Mother, but I'm going to find a home of my own, I'm tired of living in a pigsty."

He didn't have to look very far, because there was a spare sty nearby. He cleaned it, and put fresh straw in it every day. He put down an old rug he had found in the stable, and he even put up curtains! He painted a sign for his house. It said 'The Mews', with 'Percival Pig Esq' underneath it. The other pigs laughed when they saw this, but Percy didn't mind. He liked being a very clean pig and living in 'The Mews'. "Never mind the others," he told himself. "You're a very special pig."

One day Percy saw a piece of material sticking out of the mud. He got a stick and fished it out to look at it. It was a black bow tie! He took it home, washed it, dried it and then put it on. "*Very* smart!" he said to himself. Now he was a *real* gentleman – just like their Farmer!

When the other pigs saw him, they rolled around in the mud and laughed until they cried. "Who does Percy think he is?" they screamed. "He looks really funny!"

Percy decided to ignore their unkind remarks. "It doesn't matter what *they* think," he said. He put his nose high in the air and walked through the farmyard in a dignified fashion, muttering to himself.

Unfortunately, he didn't look where he was going. The next moment he fell head first into the deepest, muddiest puddle in the farmyard. "Help!" he cried, but it was too late. As he crawled out covered in thick black mud the other pigs laughed all over again. They laughed and laughed and laughed until their sides ached.

Percy didn't like this at all. He felt really silly as the mud trickled all over his skin. Then surprisingly, after the shock of falling in it, it began to feel quite nice. It was so nice that he went to find some more of that lovely mud – and rolled, and rolled, and even wallowed in it! The other pigs stared in amazement, but he didn't care.

"I've decided it's much more fun being a very *dirty* pig," laughed Percy.

The pogsogs

by Jean Doyle
illustrated by John Dyke

The pogsogs' den, deep in the fir trees, was full of noisy chatter and laughter. Marmaduke pogsog had found an empty cardboard box that morning and the pogsogs were trying to decide what to use it for. Marmaduke thought that it would make a really good store cupboard, for it was certainly big enough to house lots and lots of odds and ends. (There is nothing a pogsog likes better than a good many odds and ends!) Herman wanted to make it into a tent, while Trongo thought it would be rather nice to sleep in.

"What do you think, Ritty?" they asked Ritty, for he was the clever one and they always listened to his ideas. But Ritty yawned and closed his eyes, and refused to say anything at all.

"I'm going outside," said Trongo, putting on his coat, "to see what I can find. Coming anyone ?"

Herman and Marmaduke got their duffel coats and they all looked expectantly at Ritty.

"Might as well, I suppose," he said, opening his eyes and yawning again. Then they had to wait while he found his boots, for it was only six o'clock in the morning and bitterly cold.

The four little pogsogs shuffled along the passageways that led to the big world outside. Although none of them had ever been any farther than the firs themselves, they thought that *was* the big world! They reached the entrance to the burrows and poked their noses out, sniffing the air with their tiny noses and looking all around with their huge owl-like eyes. When you are only about seven inches high and lovely and cuddly and soft (even nicer than a teddy bear!) you have to be very careful. Everybody wants to pick you up. They got no peace at all. That was why the pogsogs usually only came out at night. It was much safer, and they liked the calm gentle light of the moon better than the harsh glare of the sun.

Of course, in the winter the sunlight was not quite so bright so they could sometimes go out during the day. Now they emerged, slowly, one by one, still looking all around, and sniffing carefully. Trongo, being the most daring, was first to dash off into the bushes, where he had spotted something shiny. Within seconds he was shovelling earth and leaves out of the way, and pulling and tugging at the treasure he had found. The others crowded round eagerly, and even Ritty was anxious to see what it was.

Herman tugged at the other pogsogs' coats suddenly.

"I can hear something!" he whispered. They all listened, lifting their brown furry heads into the air as they did so.

"Probably one of those nosy rabbits," said Trongo. "They're always interfering."

"No, no," said Herman. "It's coming from that," he pointed nervously. "That thing there." They all listened carefully to the shiny object Trongo had found. Sure enough, there was a noise coming from it. Tick a tick a tick a tick a. It frightened them a little, but since the shiny thing did not move or say anything to them, they gradually overcame their fear and crept nearer to see it better. When brave Trongo dusted the top of it with his

coat sleeve, the others gasped in terror, but still nothing happened.

"Look . . . look . . ." cried Trongo excitedly. The thing had a huge shiny face and as it made the tick a tick a sound, a little black hand moved round and round. It looked most exciting.

"What is it?" "Is it dangerous?" "Where did it come from?" "Can we move it?" They stood around chattering excitedly. Then the four of them lifted it carefully, and dragged it to the burrow. Heaving and pushing it along passageways, they made their way to the living room. Here

their squeals and shouts awoke Aunt Vim. She came bustling in, her spectacles balanced dangerously on the end of her nose.

"What's all this noise about?" she said, brushing a stray piece of fur from her face.

They showed her the shiny thing but she screamed in alarm at the sound coming from it. She jumped on the table, her pinafore over her head, and refused to move until they took it away. The pogsogs tried to calm her down, but it was no use. Aunt Vim was staying just where she was, and that was that.

"I know!" Trongo said. "Let's find Uncle Craker – he'll tell us what it is."

So Trongo, Marmaduke and Herman went off to find Uncle Craker, and Ritty stayed with Aunt Vim to protect her.

A few minutes later the three pogsogs came hurrying back, dragging Uncle Craker by the shirt sleeves. He was grumbling angrily to himself, for he really did not like young pogsogs and the noise they made. He seemed to forget that he had ever been young himself.

"*Will* you stop dragging me . . . Let me go, you naughty young pogsogs," he shouted.

"Look . . . Look . . ." they said pointing to the thing on the floor.

Uncle Craker marched up to it crossly, not a bit afraid. "Hmmmm . . . Hmm . . ." he mumbled, stroking his chin thoughtfully as he looked at it. "Just as I thought, just as I thought . . ."

"Well ? Well ?" the young pogsogs asked impatiently.

"Wait here a minute," he said, and shuffled slowly out of the room. He returned in a little while with a picture out of a magazine.

"What is Aunt Vim supposed to be doing on the table ?" he asked.

"She says we are to get rid of that thing, she's frightened of it," Trongo told him.

"Oh, don't be so silly, get down at once, Aunt Vim," Uncle Craker shouted at her. "I know just what it is, and very handy it will be too." Aunt Vim climbed down and stood behind the others, feeling a little silly. Uncle Craker opened the picture out onto the table. It showed another shiny thing just like the one they had found !

"There,' he said. "It's a watch . . . a watch just like that one."

"But what does it do?" they all asked.

"What does it do . . .? What does it do . . .? It tells the time, that's what it does. From now on we shall know when it is dinnertime, bedtime, or breakfast time without looking outside first. From now on, we shall just have to look at our watch."

He showed them all how to read it, and how to wind it. Then they hung it above the mantelpiece, and very fine it looked too. Even Aunt Vim was pleased with it.

"I know one thing . . ." Marmaduke said sleepily, as he shuffled off to bed. "I don't need to look at the watch to tell me that I'm ready for a nap!"

The other pogsogs followed him. After such a busy morning, they were *all* ready for a nap!